Alice & Lucy

Hello, I am Alice.

WILL WORK FOR

LUCY

BUNK BEDS

JAIME TEMAIRIK

Disney • HYPERION
Los Angeles   New York

For the real Alice and Lucy, and their
original creators, Martha and Adam

First Edition, July 2016
10 9 8 7 6 5 4 3 2 1
FAC-029191-16074

Printed in Malaysia

Library of Congress Cataloging-in-Publication Data

Temairik, Jaime, author, illustrator.
Alice and Lucy will work for bunk beds / Jaime Temairik.—First edition.
pages cm
Summary: "Alice and Lucy, two bear sisters, find employment at a bakery in order to raise money to buy bunk beds"—Provided by publisher.
ISBN 978-1-4847-0816-3   —ISBN 1-4847-0816-4
[1. Moneymaking projects—Fiction. 2. Bakers and bakeries—Fiction. 3. Sisters—Fiction. 4. Bears—Fiction.] I. Title.

PZ7.T2375Ali 2015
[E]—dc23   2014015779

Reinforced binding

Visit www.DisneyBooks.com

Alice and Lucy are two sisters who agree on everything.

Except maybe their favorite food.

Alice prefers peanut butter because
it only ever tastes like one thing. Peanuts.

But Lucy prefers jelly because
it can taste different every day.
There's raspberry, strawberry, apricot, you name it.

Still, the girls love doing everything together, all of the time.

Except maybe at bedtime.

One morning, Alice asks, "What's the matter, Lucy?"

"I didn't sleep very well," Lucy replies.

"Hmm . . . I did notice a few crumbs in the bed left over
from our scrumptious bedtime snacks. . . ."

Lucy isn't so sure crumbs are to blame.

"It's time for us to have separate beds," says Lucy. "We need bunk beds."

"That sounds *extravagant*," says Alice. "Besides, bunk beds cost money."

"You're right!" says Lucy. "We'll have to get jobs."

Lucky for them,
their first job interview
goes surprisingly well. . . .

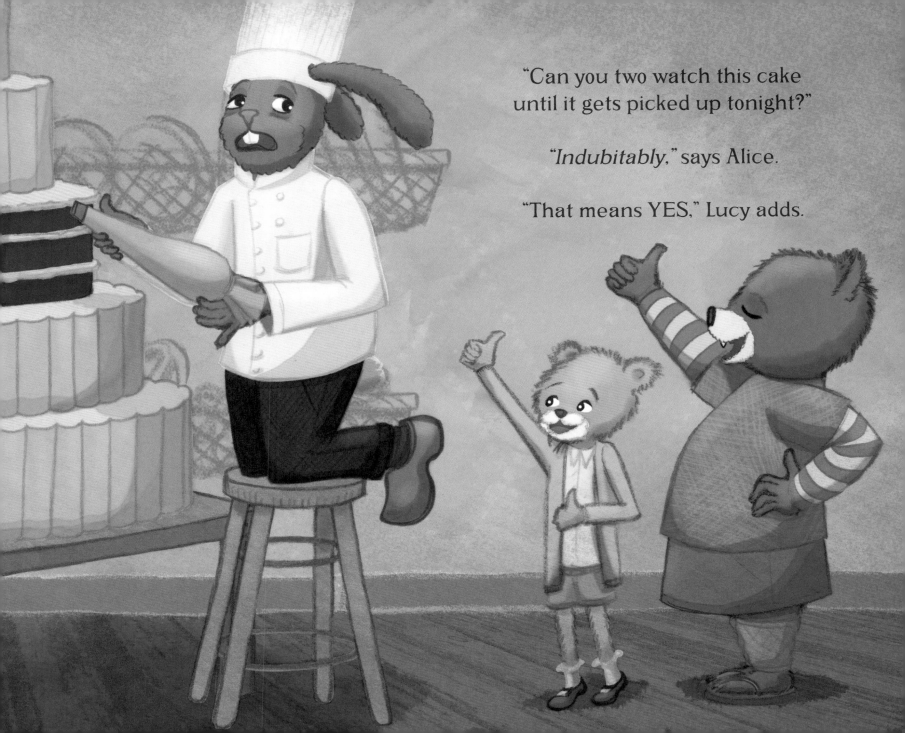

"Can you two watch this cake until it gets picked up tonight?"

"*Indubitably,*" says Alice.

"That means YES," Lucy adds.

It turns out cake babysitting is not very exciting.

"Let's have a bake-off," says Lucy.
"If I win, I get TOP BUNK in our bunk beds!"

"Well, if *I* win," replies Alice,
"we won't get bunks at all.
We'll stay together in our old bed."

Lucky for them, a bakery is a great place to have a bake-off.

"I shall make plain peanut-butter cookies," says Alice.

"I'm going to throw a bunch of jelly in the air," says Lucy, "and hope some lands in this pie dish."

 How Lucy preps

How Alice preps

How Alice measures

 How Lucy measures

 How Lucy mixes

How Alice mixes

Now, we all know if you can't say something nice,
it's best not to say anything at all.
But Alice and Lucy seem to have forgotten that.

It seems like nothing will stop Alice and Lucy from destroying the bakery

until . . .

"Your wedding cake is . . . *unavailable*," says Alice.

"Excuse me?"

"IT'S NOT READY," Lucy explains.

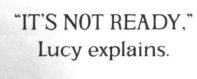

Before the customer leaves, he tells the girls the cake MUST be delivered by six o'clock, or his wedding will be ruined!

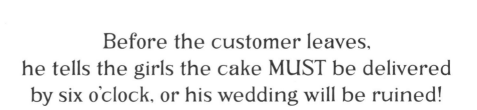

"We are doomed," says Alice.
"There's no way we can re-create the baker's cake."

Lucy is too busy eating their squished-together bake-off entries to notice.

"Mmm," says Lucy.

Alice tries some, too. "Are you thinking what I'm thinking?"

The girls get right to work.

The sign reads:

'KITCHEN'
SAFETY
• EMPLOYEES
MUST WEAR
HAIR NETS
• BUTTER IS
NOT A TOY

Alice makes sure that no feet
come into contact with any of
their ingredients while
Lucy handles all of
the heavy machinery.

The clock strikes six as Alice and Lucy present . . .

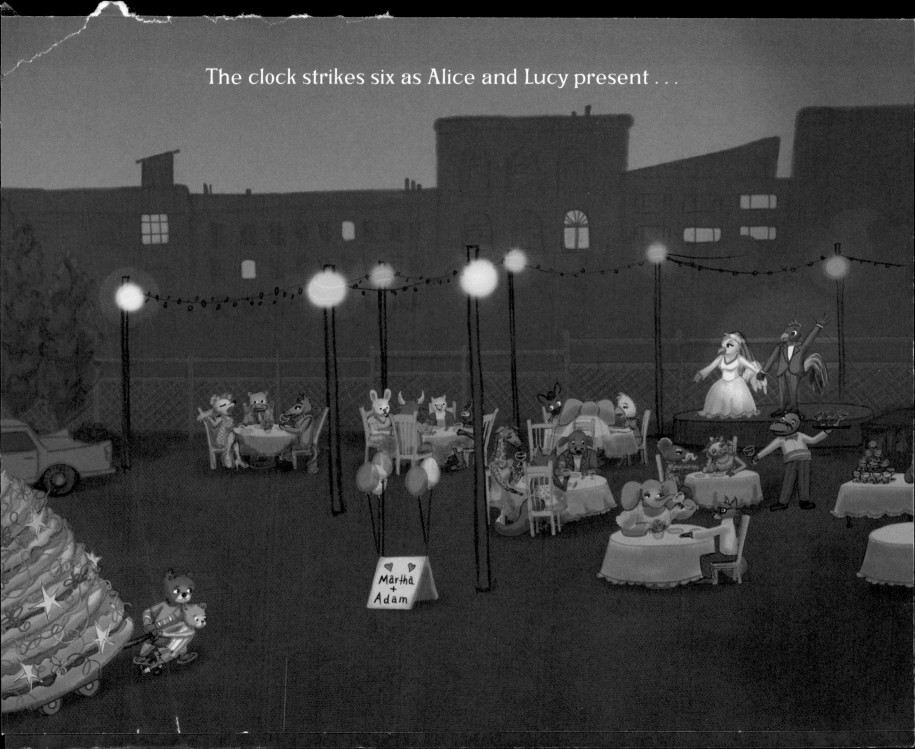

But then the baker shows up!

"I'm the big sister," says Lucy. "I'll take the blame."

"Proper sistering means we share the blame,"
says Alice.

They hear the groom shouting,
"This isn't what we ordered . . ."

"... it's better!" says the bride.

"Peanut-butter cookie cake
with six kinds of jelly filling,"
the baker says. "Who's the genius?"

The baker pays the sisters
for a job well done and asks
if they can work for him every day.

"Oh, we've conquered bakerying,"
says Alice, "so we offer you
our parting *salutations*."

"That means WE'RE OUTTA HERE!" says Lucy.

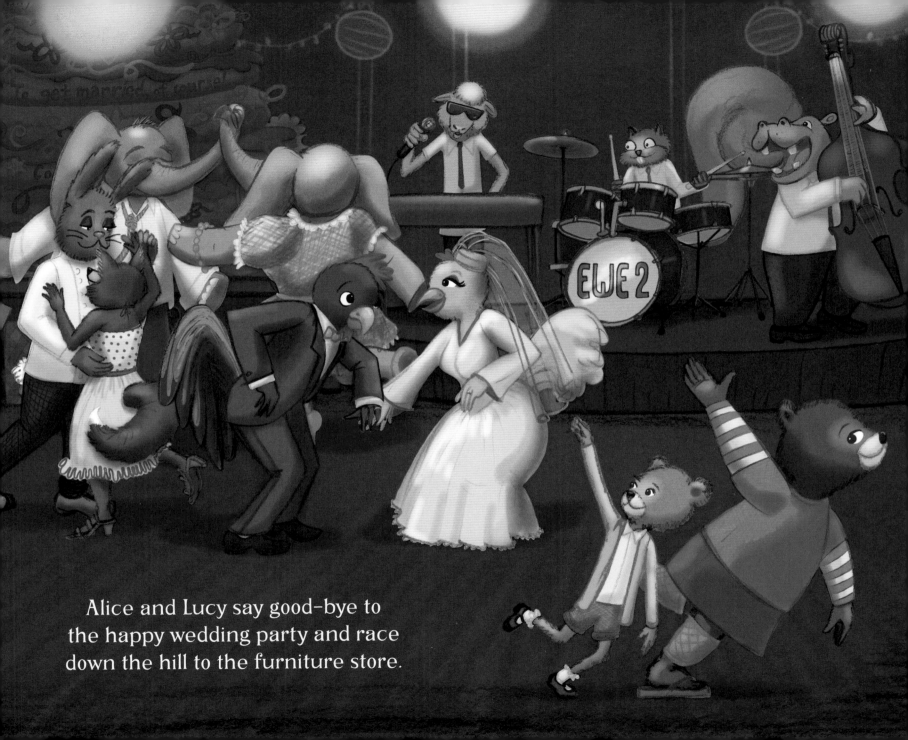

Alice and Lucy say good-bye to the happy wedding party and race down the hill to the furniture store.

Lucky for them, the store
has one bunk bed left.

Now all the girls have to do is figure out who won the bake-off. . . .

They decide it was a tie.